KU-321-544

LORNA JANE CAMPBELL

# AMELIARANNE
# KEEPS SHOP

*Told by*
Constance Heward

*Pictured by*
S. B. Pearse

GEORGE G. HARRAP & CO. LTD.
LONDON     BOMBAY     SYDNEY

AMELIARANNE Stiggins was sad.
Though spring was in the air and
the bluebells out and all the birds
singing, Ameliaranne could think of
nothing but — BOOTS ! And even
the twenty-five ringlets which bobbed
about her neck looked sad and limp.

The Squire was giving a treat to the village children next week. A green and yellow bus was coming from town to take them to the bluebell woods, and after they had picked as many bluebells as they could carry they were to have tea in Farmer Brown's barn, and then they were going to look for eggs, and feed the calves, and play hide-and-seek in the farmyard.

When the invitation came for the six Stigginses, Mrs Stiggins got out the family's boots.

" Ameliaranne and Richard and Rosabel can go," she said, " but Jenny and Joey and Wee William must stop at home. Their boots are through and not worth mending, and there'll be no money to buy new ones this month, and trapesing about that farmyard would finish 'em *out and out !* "

Now, while Ameliaranne was still wrapped in sadness because of the fate of the three youngest Stigginses, Mrs Poppet walked in, and when Mrs Stiggins saw the smile on her plump face she put down her iron—she took in washing—and said, "Your Johnnie's coming home!"

And Mrs Poppet replied, "I'm just off to town to meet him, and I want your Ameliaranne to come and mind the shop."

Little lights danced in Ameliaranne's eyes. She had helped Mrs Poppet before, but never had she dreamed of anything so delightful and delicious as keeping shop by herself.

"Ameliaranne's to be trusted," said Mrs Poppet, "and she can bring her curl-rags and stay the night."

Mrs Poppet's shop stood all alone on a big piece of waste ground. Behind it were the kitchen and the bedrooms, like a bungalow, and over the shop-door was printed this sign:

JOHN & PATIENCE POPPET

This was because her sailor son Johnnie had sent the money from the other end of the world for Mrs Poppet, whose name was Patience, to build the shop.

Mrs Poppet sold candles and cheese and picture-postcards, and lard and reels of cotton, and humbugs and jujubes and elastic.

Ameliaranne tied a large checked apron round her waist, and Mrs Poppet trotted off with happiness shining all over her plump person, calling as she went :

" Ameliaranne, get two pounds of sausages from the butcher's for supper, and don't expect us till you see us. Ta-ta ! "

Mrs Poppet had scarcely gone when the little bell on the shop-door tinkled and Miss McCrustie came in. She had met Mrs Poppet going down the road, and when she found Ameliaranne Stiggins keeping shop she was greatly offended that she had not been asked to do it, and she flounced out without buying anything.

The next customers were Mrs Lemon and Miss Quince. They would have loved to keep shop for Mrs Poppet, and when they saw who was doing so they asked very sourly for two ounces of butter and a quarter of lard, and poor Ameliaranne's fingers seemed to be all thumbs as she weighed them out.

When the children heard that Ameliaranne Stiggins was keeping shop they came in dozens for hap'orths of acid-drops and penn'orths of humbugs, and Ameliaranne leaned over the counter and said, " Now, love," in Mrs Poppet's own manner.

She gave exact weight and held the paper bags by the two top corners, twirling them over and over as if she had kept shop for forty years.

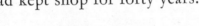

When the five little Stigginses came
with a penny among them Ameliaranne
opened the box with the jujube babies
labelled " Six a Penny."

" There, my dears," she said ; " one
for each of you and one for your good,
hard-working mother."

And the little Stigginses went out of
the shop with their hands over their
mouths to hide their giggles.

All day the shop-bell tinkled and Ameliaranne ate her dinner in snatches, and in the drawer under the counter there were half-crowns and shillings, and sixpences and threepenny-bits, and pennies and ha'pennies, and even pound notes and ten-shilling notes, and Ameliaranne said with a long, long sigh :

" Mother could buy *dozens* of *boots* with all this money."

When it grew dusk the shopkeeper lighted the lamp, and when the cuckoo in the kitchen clock shouted nine she showed the last customer out, and was turning the key in the lock when

The door was pushed open again and a great big sailorman walked in and said :

"Hullo, little girl ! Are you keeping shop ? I'm Mrs Poppet's Johnnie, all the way from the other end of nowhere."

But Ameliaranne saw by the light from the lamp that his eyes were brown, and she knew that Mrs Poppet's Johnnie's eyes were as blue as the billowy sea.

So she told him he must have missed his mother in the town, but she'd be sure to be home on the ten o'clock train, and would he be so obliging as to step down the street to the butcher's and buy two pounds of sausages for supper, and would he hurry or the shop would be shut ?

The sailor took the half-crown she offered and said he could do with his supper, and Ameliaranne peeked round the door as he went, and she knew for sure and certain that he was not a sailor because he walked like an ordinary person, and didn't roll from side to side as real sailors do.

Ameliaranne looked wildly round the shop, and she lifted the lid of the big stone jar of pickled onions and *plump, splash, splosh !*—in went the half-crowns and shillings, and sixpences and three-penny-bits, and pennies and ha'pennies, and instead of being half full of pickled onions that jar seemed to be full right to the very brim.

But the pound notes and ten-shilling notes were still in Ameliaranne's hand.

She ran to the kitchen, but there was no safe place to hide them.

She ran to the bedroom. On the dressing - table were her twenty-five curl-rags, which she had long ago learnt to put in for herself.

Her eyes danced, and she began to twist the rags into her hair with lightning fingers.

When the sailor came back with the sausages Ameliaranne had lighted the lamp in the kitchen, and every now and then she gave her head a little sharp shake because the curl-rags tickled the back of her neck.

As the sailor went into the shop to look round she called gloomily, " Times are very bad, Mr Johnnie. No money coming in at all these days," and then

She popped the sausages into the frying-pan, and as they sizzled and spluttered she shivered and shook for joy that she had filled the pickled-onion jar to the very brim, and that she had put her hair into curl-rags.

The sailor came back and poked into all the corners of the kitchen, and then he went on to the bedrooms, and Ameliaranne could hear him opening the cupboards and rummaging in the drawers, and she giggled as if she had a great joke, and just then came the sound of the ten o'clock train puffing loudly into the station and

Out ran the sailor, away through the shop and down the road as if he couldn't run fast enough to meet his mother, but he ran *away from the station*, and while Ameliaranne stood in the shop with the frying-pan and the fork in her hand

Mrs Poppet came walking in with a great big breezy sailor, who picked Ameliaranne up, frying-pan and all, and kissed her.

Ameliaranne said, " *Lock the door!* "
and she popped the frying-pan down on
the counter and gasped out the story
while she brought out handfuls of half-
crowns and shillings, and sixpences and
threepenny-bits, and pennies and ha'-
pennies, from the bottom of the jar of
pickled onions.

Then she bent her head, and though her ringlets were done in curl-*rags* on the crown, the last row round her neck was screwed up in pound notes and ten-shilling ones, and when Mrs Poppet took them out ever so carefully there was six pounds ten on the counter.

They had supper then, and Ameliaranne told the story all over again, and
when she came to the end of it she
began at the beginning once more, and
Sailor Johnnie said :

" Hey, my hearty, you've saved the
ship to-night from a bold, bad buc-
caneer ! "

The next morning when Mrs Poppet and Johnnie saw Ameliaranne off at the door Johnnie said, " Ameliaranne Stiggins, don't you go leaving all your old curl-papers behind," and he put one of them into her hand.

Ameliaranne ran home so fast that
when she got there she could only pant
out, " B-b-boots for J-janey and J-joey
and W-w-wee W-illiam ! " as she waved
the curl-paper in front of Mrs Stiggins,
who couldn't see a curl-paper because
she saw a pound note.

The sun shone and the sky was blue on the day of the picnic, and Ameliaranne and the five little Stigginses rode gaily in the green and yellow bus to the bluebell woods.

After tea in the barn with home-made bread and golden butter, and new-laid eggs and strawberry jam, they played in the farmyard, which was as dirty as farmyards generally are.

But that didn't matter, for Jenny and Joey and Wee William wore strong new boots bought with one of Ameliar-anne's costly curl-papers.

*First published 1928*
*by* GEORGE G. HARRAP & CO. LTD.
*39-41 Parker Street, Kingsway, London, W.C.2*
*Reprinted January 1933*

*Printed in Great Britain by Morrison & Gibb Ltd.*
*London and Edinburgh*